Dear Parent,

Thunderstorms can be frightening to little ones. The roar of the thunder . . . the howl of the wind . . . the jagged streaks of lightning as they race across the sky.

Now, in one delightfully-told-and-illustrated book, children learn that fear of thunderstorms can be overcome—and even turned into delicious celebrations!

Using adventures from her own childhood with her Russian Babushka (grandmother), Patricia Polacco recalls the day she and her grandmother prepared for a fierce thunderstorm by baking a special thunder cake. As they scurried about the farm collecting ingredients for the cake, the little girl faced many new challenges that taught her just how brave she really was.

From the minute you and your child open this book, you'll be caught up with the heartwarming story, as well as the beautiful pencil/color wash illustrations. These fresh and dramatic details have already won this author/illustrator a 1989 International Reading Association Award for an earlier book, *Rechenka's Eggs*.

Take a few minutes now to share this story with your child. And the next time a thunderstorm threatens, open to the last page of the story and follow the recipe for making your *own* Thunder Cake. Enjoy!

Sincerely,

Elizabeth Isele
Executive Editor
Weekly Reader Books

Weekly Reader Children's Book Club Presents

Thunder cake

PATRICIA POLACCO

PHILOMEL BOOKS

NEW YORK

For my Babushka Carlé, with love

This book is a presentation of Weekly Reader Books. Weekly Reader Books offers book clubs
for children from preschool through high school. For further information write to: **Weekly
Reader Books**, 4343 Equity Drive, Columbus, Ohio 43228.

Published by arrangement with Philomel Books, a division of The Putnam & Grosset Group.
Weekly Reader is a federally registered trademark of Field Publications.

Library of Congress Cataloging-in-Publication Data
Polacco, Patricia.
Thunder cake/Patricia Polacco.
   p.   cm.
Summary: Grandma finds a way to dispel her grandchild's fear of thunderstorms. ISBN 0-399-
22231-6 (1. Thunderstorms—Fiction. 2. Fear—Fiction. 3. Grandmothers—Fiction.) I. Title.
PZ7.P75186Th   1990   (E)—dc20 89-33405 CIP AC

First impression

On sultry summer days at my grandma's farm in Michigan, the air gets damp and heavy. Stormclouds drift low over the fields. Birds fly close to the ground. The clouds glow for an instant with a sharp, crackling light, and then a roaring, low, tumbling sound of thunder makes the windows shudder in their panes. The sound used to scare me when I was little. I loved to go to Grandma's house (Babushka, as I used to call my grandma, had come from Russia years before), but I feared Michigan's summer storms. I feared the sound of thunder more than anything. I always hid under the bed when the storm moved near the farmhouse.

This is the story of how my grandma—my Babushka—helped me overcome my fear of thunderstorms.

Grandma looked at the horizon, drew a deep breath and said, "This is Thunder Cake baking weather, all right. Looks like a storm coming to me."

"Child, you come out from under that bed. It's only thunder you're hearing," my grandma said.

The air was hot, heavy and damp. A loud clap of thunder shook the house, rattled the windows and made me grab her close.

"Steady, child," she cooed. "Unless you let go of me, we won't be able to make a Thunder Cake today!"

"Thunder Cake?" I stammered as I hugged her even closer.

"Don't pay attention to that old thunder, except to see how close the storm is getting. When you see the lightning, start counting... real slow. When you hear the thunder, stop counting. That number is how many miles away the storm is. Understand?" she asked. "We need to know how far away the storm is, so we have time to make the cake and get it into the oven before the storm comes, or it won't be real Thunder Cake."

Her eyes surveyed the black clouds a way off in the distance. Then she strode into the kitchen. Her worn hands pulled a thick book from the shelf above the woodstove.

"Let's find that recipe, child," she crowed as she lovingly fingered the grease-stained pages to a creased spot.

"Here it is... Thunder Cake!"

She carefully penned the ingredients on a piece of notepaper. "Now let's gather all the things we'll need!" she exclaimed as she scurried toward the back door.

We were by the barn door when a huge bolt of lightning flashed. I started counting, like Grandma told me to, "1–2–3–4–5–6–7–8–9–10."

Then the thunder ROARED!

"Ten miles…it's ten miles away," Grandma said as she looked at the sky. "About an hour away, I'd say. You'll have to hurry, child. Gather them eggs careful-like," she said.

Eggs from mean old Nellie Peck Hen. I was scared. I knew she would try to peck me.

"I'm here, she won't hurt you. Just get them eggs," Grandma said softly.

The lightning flashed again. "1–2–3–4–5–6–7–8–9" I counted.

"Nine miles," Grandma reminded me.

Milk was next. Milk from old Kick Cow. As Grandma milked her, Kick Cow turned and looked mean, right at me. I was scared. She looked so big.

ZIP went the lightning. "1–2–3–4–5–6–7–8" I counted.

BAROOOOOOOOOM went the thunder.

"Eight miles, child," Grandma croaked. "Now we have to get chocolate and sugar and flour from the dry shed."

I was scared as we walked down the path from the farmhouse through Tangleweed Woods to the dry shed. Suddenly the lightning slit the sky!

"1–2–3–4–5–6–7" I counted.

BOOOOOOM BA-BOOOOOOM, crashed the thunder. It scared me a lot, but I kept walking with Grandma.

Another jagged edge of lightning flashed as I crept into the dry shed! "1–2–3–4–5–6" I counted.

CRACKLE, CRACKLE BOOOOOOOM, KA-BOOOOOM, the thunder bellowed. It was dark and I was scared.

"I'm here, child," Grandma said softly from the doorway. "Hurry now, we haven't got much time. We've got everything but the secret ingredient."

"Three overripe tomatoes and some strawberries," Grandma whispered as she squinted at the list.

I climbed up high on the trellis. The ground looked a long way down. I was scared.

"I'm here, child," she said. Her voice was steady and soft. "You won't fall."

I reached three luscious tomatoes while she picked strawberries. Lightning again!

"1–2–3–4–5" I counted.

KA-BANG BOOOOOOOOAROOOOM, the thunder growled.

We hurried back to the house and the warm kitchen, and we measured the ingredients. I poured them into the mixing bowl while Grandma mixed. I churned butter for the frosting and melted chocolate. Finally, we poured the batter into the cake pans and put them into the oven together.

Lightning lit the kitchen! I only counted to three and the thunder RRRRUMBLED and CRASHED.

"Three miles away," Grandma said, "and the cake is in the oven. We made it! We'll have a real Thunder Cake!"

As we waited for the cake, Grandma looked out the window for a long time. "Why, you aren't afraid of thunder. You're too brave!" she said as she looked right at me.

"I'm not brave, Grandma," I said. "I was under the bed! Remember?"

"But you got out from under it," she answered, "and
you got eggs from mean old Nellie Peck Hen,
you got milk from old Kick Cow,
you went through Tangleweed Woods to the dry shed,
you climbed the trellis in the barnyard.
From where I sit, only a very brave person could have done all them things!"

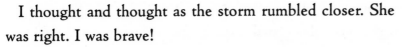

I thought and thought as the storm rumbled closer. She was right. I was brave!

"Brave people can't be afraid of a sound, child," she said as we spread out the tablecloth and set the table. When we were done, we hurried into the kitchen to take the cake out of the oven. After the cake had cooled, we frosted it.

Just then the lightning flashed, and this time it lit the whole sky.

Even before the last flash had faded, the thunder ROLLED, BOOOOOMED, CRASHED, and BBBBAAAAARRRRR-OOOOOOOOMMMMMMMMMED just above us. The storm was here!

"Perfect," Grandma cooed, "just perfect." She beamed as she added the last strawberry to the glistening chocolate frosting on top of our Thunder Cake.

As rain poured down on our roof, Grandma cut a wedge for each of us. She poured us steaming cups of tea from the samovar.

When the thunder ROARED above us so hard it shook the windows and rattled the dishes in the cupboards, we just smiled and ate our Thunder Cake.

From that time on, I never feared the voice of thunder again.

My Grandma's Thunder Cake

Cream together, one at a time
- 1 cup shortening
- 1¾ cup sugar
- 1 teaspoon vanilla
- 3 eggs, separated
  (Blend yolks in. Beat whites until they are stiff, then fold in.)

- 1 cup cold water
- ⅓ cup pureed tomatoes

Sift together
- 2½ cups cake flour
- ½ cup dry cocoa
- 1½ teaspoons baking soda
- 1 teaspoon salt

Mix dry mixture into creamy mixture.
Bake in two greased and floured 8½-inch round pans at 350° for 35 to 40 minutes.
Frost with chocolate butter frosting. Top with strawberries.